RANSOM

Berry

D0720453

SADDLEBACK
EDUCATIONAL PUBLISHING

T H E   H E I G H T S®

Blizzard	**Ransom**
Camp	River
Crash	Sail
Creature	Score
Dam	Shelter
Dive	Swamp
Heist	Treasure
Jump	Tsunami
Mudslide	Twister
Neptune	Wild

Original text by Ed Hansen
Adapted by Mary Kate Doman

SADDLEBACK
EDUCATIONAL PUBLISHING
www.sdlback.com

ISBN-13: 978-1-62250-047-5
ISBN-10: 1-62250-047-4
eBook: 978-1-61247-705-3

Printed in the U.S.A.

19 18 17 16 15   3 4 5 6 7

Chapter 1

Antonio was racing to get ready. It was the first track meet of the year. And he was late.

"Hurry up, Antonio," Ana yelled. "You're going to miss the bus!"

"One minute, Mom," shouted Antonio. "I can't find my shoes!"

"They're by the front door," Ana called out. "Let's go!"

Antonio ran down the stairs. He

grabbed a banana. Then he put on his shoes.

Lilia was waiting for him. She'd been ready for over an hour.

It was a sunny Saturday morning. Antonio and Lilia were on the Rockdale Heights track team. They had a meet at Newport High in the afternoon.

Ana drove them to school. The team met in the school parking lot. They were all taking a bus to Newport. It was about an hour away.

"Sorry we can't make the meet today," Ana said. "Your dad and I have to talk with the builder. But we'll be at the next one."

"That's okay, Mom," Lilia said. "We have a lot of meets left."

"Good luck!" Ana shouted. Then she drove away.

The kids climbed aboard the bus. The coaches checked off their names as they got on.

"Everybody's here," Coach Rome said. "Let's go!"

Coach Fine, the girls' coach, gave everyone a pep talk. The Heights had a great track team. They all worked hard. They wanted to win.

At Newport High, Coaches Rome and Fine led the kids in warm-ups.

The meet went great. Rockdale Heights won. Lilia and Antonio won their races too. It was going to be a good season for the Heights track team. They even had a shot at the state championship.

The team boarded the bus to go home. The coaches made sure no one was left behind. At four o'clock the bus left Newport High.

The bus should have arrived at Rockdale Heights at five o'clock. But it didn't. Some of the parents were worried. They called their kids' cell phones. But they all went right to voicemail.

Two hours later, parents started to panic. They called the police. They looked everywhere between Rockdale and Newport. But there was no sign of the bus.

Everyone was scared and confused. A bus with over fifty people on it had vanished.

Chapter 2

There was no sign of the kids all night. Fear and panic swept through the Heights. Parents begged the police to do more.

Then the chief received an e-mail. It read:

We have the bus. The kids are safe—for now. Get us two million dollars in unmarked bills. And you'll get them back.

We'll contact you in twenty-four hours. Once we have the money, we'll tell you where the kids are. Here's proof that we have them. We're not playing games. If you want to see these kids alive, you must follow our instructions!

The chief stared at a photo of the terrified track team. Then he made a decision. Chief Vega called the FBI. A town meeting was set up at the high school. The school was full of parents, police, and FBI agents.

The chief was worried. They'd have to pay the ransom. It was too risky not to. Hopefully the kidnappers would keep their promise.

"We're doing everything we can to find the kids," Chief Vega said. "We're getting the money ready too. We have twenty-four hours to find them. If not, we have to do what they say."

No one in the crowd argued. Saving the kids was the most important thing.

Rafael Silva talked to Chief Vega.

"Antonio and Lilia are on that bus," Rafael said. "I want to help. Tell me what to do."

"I know, Rafael," the chief replied. "But there's nothing you can do. I'll call you if I need you."

The Silvas were scared and upset. "Maybe the best thing I can do is stay at home with Ana," Rafael thought. "But it's hard to just wait for news."

"Go home. Everyone needs to sit tight," said the chief.

The next day Chief Vega needed fresh air. So he took a walk. This was the worst thing that had ever happened in the Heights. So many kids were in danger. They had searched all night for the bus. There wasn't even one clue.

The FBI believed it was best to pay the ransom. The chief agreed.

He stopped in a deli. He needed more coffee. The deli's phone rang.

"Hey, Chief, the phone is for you," the clerk said.

The chief blinked. Then he grabbed the phone.

"Do you have the money?" a voice said.

Chief Vega was shocked. No one knew where he was. How did the kidnappers know? "They must be watching me," the chief thought. "They're smart. We can't trace the call from here."

"Yes, we have the money," the chief answered.

"Good. Now listen carefully," the voice said. "There is a blue bag behind the police station. Near the woods. Put the money in that bag. Then have someone deliver the money. Do not use anyone connected with the police or FBI. Do you understand?"

"Yes," Chief Vega said.

"At five this afternoon, I'll call the station with instructions. Once I get the money, I'll tell you where the kids are. But I'm warning you. No tricks!

The kids are fine, now," said the voice. "But they won't be if you don't listen!"

The line went dead. Chief Vega ran back to the station. He found the blue bag. Then he called Rafael Silva.

"I need your help, Rafael," Chief Vega said. "How fast can you get here?"

Chapter 3

Rafael was at the police station fifteen minutes later.

"Here I am," Rafael yelled. "What do you need me to do?"

"We've heard from the kidnappers," the chief said. "They're calling us again at five. They'll give us instructions for delivering the ransom. They don't want a police officer to do it. Will you do it?"

"Of course," Rafael said.

"Thanks," Chief Vega said. "Come meet the rest of the team. Then we'll go over the plan."

Rafael looked around the room. He saw a lot of people he knew.

"They won't give us the drop-off site on the first call. They never do," the chief said. "They'll make Rafael go to a few places. Officers will be all over town. Hopefully some of you will be close to the drop site. Rafael will wear a wire. And a GPS tracker. We'll know where he is at all times."

The meeting ended. All the officers changed into street clothes. They spread out around town. The chief gave Rafael a wire and GPS device.

"Remember, we'll be able to hear you at all times," said the chief.

The blue bag was at Rafael's feet. It was filled with two million dollars.

The phone rang at five on the dot.

"Go to the bus stop at Main and Elm. Be there in ten minutes. Do not drive. And come alone," the voice said.

"Hurry up," Chief Vega said. "It's about a ten-minute walk to that stop. We'll be watching you. Good luck!"

"Are the kids okay?" Rafael thought. "Will the police catch these guys? Can the kidnappers see me right now?" He didn't have any answers.

Rafael reached the bus stop. He heard a phone ringing. Taped under a bench, he found a cell phone. He grabbed it.

"Hello," Rafael said.

"So far, so good," the voice said. "Keep this cell phone. Get on the next bus. Go stand by the back doors." The call ended.

"I'm getting on the next bus," Rafael said out loud.

"Hang in there, Rafael," the chief said. "I've got officers everywhere. They will be near you."

Rafael got on the next bus. It was rush hour. So it was very crowded. The phone rang.

"We know you're wearing a wire," said the voice. "Don't tell the police we know. Do you understand?"

"Yes, I understand," Rafael replied.

"Good," the voice continued. "Put the bag down on the floor."

Rafael did as he was told.

"Keep talking to me. Pretend that nothing is happening," said the voice. "We know who you are. We know your kids are on the track team."

Rafael was stunned. "How do you know me? Where are my kids?" he asked.

The bus was filling up with more people. More people were getting off. Someone grabbed his bag and replaced it with another. The bags looked the same. But the bag with the money was gone.

Rafael knew what was happening. But he didn't know what to do.

"Stay on this bus. Don't get off until Middle Street," the voice said. "Then your work is done. We're watching you. Keep your mouth shut until you get off the bus. If you say one word about what happened? You'll never see Antonio or Lilia again," the voice threatened.

Rafael knew that he couldn't warn the police. He'd put the kids in danger. He had to follow the kidnappers' instructions. The money was gone.

"My next stop is Middle Street," Rafael said into the microphone.

A half hour later, Rafael got off the bus.

"Chief Vega, it's a trick! They already took the money," Rafael yelled. "They're long gone by now!"

Chapter 4

Chief Vega was mad! Officers searched the bus. They examined the cell phone. But there were no clues. No one had any idea of what to do next.

Then the phone rang.

"Listen carefully," the voice said. "The kids are locked in an old ship. It's called *Leto*. It's tied up in the harbor."

Then the phone went dead.

"We've got them!" Chief Vega shouted.

The harbor was fifty miles away in Newport. Officers nearby were there in minutes. The *Leto* was at the end of an old pier. It had been empty for years.

Police opened the hold. The missing track team, coaches, and bus driver looked up at them. Some kids cheered. Other kids cried. The officers went right to work. They took everyone to the hospital.

The good news traveled fast. The teens had been found! Everyone was safe and healthy. Parents sped toward the hospital.

The next morning the police station was crazy. Everyone was

happy the teens were safe. But a crime had been committed. And the criminals got away with two million dollars! Now the police needed to catch the kidnappers. And they needed to get the ransom back.

They searched the ship for clues. How did the bus get there unseen?

First the bus driver and two coaches were questioned. Then the kids. Everyone's story was the same. Two men in ski masks pushed their way onto the bus. They each had a gun. The coaches were tied up. One man pointed his gun at the kids. He went around and took everyone's cell phones. The other man pointed his gun at the bus driver. He gave the driver directions.

They drove for fifteen minutes. Then they came to a huge truck. It was carrying a large shipping container. The bus went up a ramp at the back of the truck. It vanished into the open container. Then everything went dark.

"Well," Chief Vega said. "Now we know how the bus got to the harbor without being seen!"

Chapter 5

For days the police looked at everything connected with the case. They dusted for fingerprints. They questioned rush hour bus passengers.

"These guys are very smart," Chief Vega thought. "We've got to be even smarter to catch them."

Investigators went over the school bus and shipping container. But the police had little to go on.

Chief Vega started to think the case would never be solved.

For some of the students the kidnapping was a bad dream. For others it was a nightmare. The school added special counselors to the staff.

Antonio and Lilia dealt with the kidnapping very well. It was a terrifying experience. But both teenagers were doing fine.

Rafael and Ana watched the late news. Lilia sat down next to them.

"What's wrong?" Ana asked. "Are you having trouble sleeping?"

"I was just dreaming about being on the bus," said Lilia. "I remembered something. It may not be important. But the police said even the littlest thing may help."

"What is it?" Rafael asked.

"It happened just before the two men left the ship. One of them called the other 'mate.' I remember thinking 'mate' was a weird thing to call someone. But like I said, it's nothing big," said Lilia.

"Maybe. But maybe not," Rafael said. "Let's stop by the police station tomorrow. You can tell Chief Vega about it."

The next morning Rafael took Lilia to the police station. Lilia told the chief what she told her parents. Chief Vega listened closely. Then he thanked her.

"Lilia," Chief Vega said. "Let's keep this information between us."

"Sure. No problem," Lilia replied.

Rafael dropped Lilia off at school. Then he went back to the police station.

"What do you think?" Rafael asked. "Does Lilia's information help?"

"Lilia's right," the chief replied. "The word 'mate' isn't common around here. It's used in England and Australia."

"Is anyone in town from there?" Rafael asked.

"I don't know," the chief replied. "But if there is, we'll find him. The principal is getting me info on the school staff. Maybe we'll find what we need there."

The chief didn't tell anyone about what Lilia remembered. He knew it was a long shot. But he couldn't be too careful. He spent hours looking at the school staff records. Then something caught his eye. He was looking at the file on Ken Cruise.

Mr. Cruise was the shop teacher. He'd been working at the school four years. Cruise was from Sydney, Australia.

The chief assigned two officers to watch Ken Cruise.

"I want to know where he goes. Who he sees," Chief Vega said. "And don't let him know we're watching him."

Chapter 6

Back at the harbor, FBI agents searched the waterfront. The kidnappers had used a crane to lift the shipping container onto the ship.

The pier had been closed for a year. It was only used to dock old ships. No one saw anything. But to use a crane, they would have needed a crane operator. So police questioned all of the crane operators on the docks. They had no suspects.

Back in the Heights, the officers watching Ken Cruise didn't have a hard job. Ken got to school at seven in the morning. He left at four in the afternoon. The first two nights he didn't leave his house. But on the third night, he went to a diner.

Another man met him there. They were yelling at each other. But the police couldn't hear. They took down the second man's license plate number.

The officers ran the plate number. Then they called the chief.

Rafael's birthday was in two weeks. Antonio had been building

him a small bookcase in shop
class. He was worried it wouldn't
be finished in time. He asked Mr.
Cruise if he could finish it after
school.

"Do you think the police will
ever catch the kidnappers?" Antonio
asked as he sanded the wood.

"I hope so," answered Mr. Cruise.
"But I heard they don't have any
clues."

"They have one," Antonio said.

"How do you know?" asked Mr.
Cruise.

"My dad is friends with Chief
Vega," Antonio replied. "I heard them
talking."

"I wonder what it could be,"
mused Mr. Cruise.

Antonio was finally putting the first coat of paint on the bookcase.

"You're doing a great job on this project," Mr. Cruise said. "I think your dad will like it."

"Thanks," Antonio replied. "I think he'll like it too."

"Speaking of your dad, what clue did he think the chief needed to hear? ... I think it would be great if they caught those guys," Mr. Cruise said.

"Yeah, me too!" Antonio exclaimed. "The clue came from my sister. She heard one of the kidnappers call the other one 'mate.' Now the police think the kidnappers are from England or Australia. I bet they'll find them soon."

Ken Cruise froze. He couldn't talk. He needed time to think.

Antonio didn't notice his teacher acting strangely. He put away the paint. Cleaned the brushes. And put away his tools. The bookcase would need another coat of paint. And then he would seal it. It would be ready in time for his father's birthday. Antonio was happy.

Chapter 7

Ken called his brother, Mark. Then he called a man named Joe Bush. He left the same message for both men. "We need to talk," Ken said. "Meet me at the diner tonight at seven."

Both men met Ken at the diner.

"What's wrong?" Mark Cruise asked.

"We have a big problem,"
Ken said. "The police know the
kidnappers are from Australia."

"How do they know that?" Joe
Bush asked.

"Some kid heard one of us call
the other 'mate.' She thought it was
strange," Ken said. "So she told the
police."

Joe Bush turned red. He was
mad.

"We pulled off the perfect crime.
Then you blew it by calling each
other 'mate.' You're both idiots!"
shouted Joe.

"We need a new plan," Mark said.
"We can't sit around here for the
next six months. Let's split up the
money. Let's get out of here now!"

"I'm not going anywhere," said Joe. "I'm not from Australia. You two can take your cut of the money. Do what you want. I'm staying put!"

They had hidden the money in Joe's basement. The three men didn't trust each other. They made sure no one could run off with the money. There were three strong locks on the basement door. Each man held a key to one lock.

Chapter 8

It was almost nine that night when they got to Joe's. Each man opened a lock. The money was still in the blue bag. They got to work dividing the ransom.

"Almost seven hundred thou each. Not bad for a night's work," Mark said.

"Not bad if we don't get caught," Joe added. "Where are you guys going?"

"We're not sure yet," Ken answered.

"Well, if you get caught? Don't rat me out," said Joe. "You'll be sorry if you do!"

Mark and Ken Cruise had to get out of town. They decided to leave the country.

"Let's go to Canada. Now," Mark said. "We can be in Toronto by morning."

The next morning Chief Vega met with the FBI. He told them what he found out about Ken and Mark Cruise. They decided to bring them in right away.

The chief sent out two police units. He sent one to the high school.

The other he sent to the lumberyard. Mark was a crane operator there. Both units found out the same thing. Neither Cruise brother showed up for work.

Chief Vega was very angry. It looked like the brothers had already left town. He wished he'd acted sooner. But there was no way they could have known they were suspects.

The chief wanted to search their houses. He called a judge for two search warrants.

Chapter 9

Chief Vega and his officers looked around Ken Cruise's house. It was clear he left in a hurry. The rooms were a mess.

"Most of the drawers and closets are empty," the chief said. "I don't think this guy is coming back."

Police officers at Mark Cruise's house found the same thing. It was clear. Both men were on the run!

An APB (all-points bulletin) was put out for both men. The police department released their descriptions. Plus their license plate numbers. And their car makes and models.

But hours earlier Mark and Ken had made it to Canada. They paid cash for a hotel. Then they got some breakfast. Every time they bought something, they paid in cash. There was no way for the police to track them.

The police and FBI didn't have any luck. Their only suspects had disappeared. But how did they know they were suspects? The chief thought someone must have tipped them off. That was the only way to explain their fast exit.

Police use phone records to get information. This case was no different. They searched Ken Cruise's cell phone bills. The day before he disappeared, Ken made two calls. He made one call to his brother. And the other to a man named Joe Bush.

"It's the third guy from the diner!" Chief Vega said. "We ran his license plate. This guy may be involved."

Then the chief had a thought. "They needed a third man to drive the truck. The other two guys were busy on the bus. This may be our lucky break."

Chapter 10

Phone records showed that Joe Bush might have been involved in the kidnapping. Joe had called Mark. And Joe had called Ken. A search warrant was issued for his house. When the officers arrived, no one was home.

The officers broke down the door and searched the house from top to bottom. They saw two locks on the ground by the basement door. There was one lock on the door too. They cut the lock off. Right away officers found the blue bag with some money inside.

"One down. Two to go!" Chief Vega shouted.

Two officers waited in the dark for Joe Bush. Three hours later Joe came home. Joe was arrested as soon as he walked in the door. He couldn't believe it. He had been so careful.

Chief Vega questioned Joe for hours. But he wasn't getting anywhere.

"Where are the Cruise brothers?" asked the chief. "You should cooperate. Tell us. Maybe the DA will go easy on you. And make a deal."

"And for the tenth time, I don't know!" shouted Joe.

It looked like the Cruise brothers got away.

Car thefts were on the rise in Canada. The Canadian police were trying to crack down. They were checking license plates. Officers had lists of missing and stolen cars.

Two Canadian officers were patrolling a shopping center in Toronto. They were checking out the license plates of cars in the lot. One officer noticed a black van with an American license plate.

"I want to check out that van," one officer said. "It seems suspicious. It has been there for too long."

The officers looked at the plates as the Cruise brothers left a store. The plates matched an APB. By the time the Cruise brothers saw the police, it was too late. They were arrested in the parking lot.

Thirty minutes later an officer from Toronto called Rockdale Heights. He told Chief Vega the good news.

"Two of my men just caught Ken and Mark Cruise," the officer said. "Thanks to the APB you put out. We found over a million dollars cash in their hotel room. These are definitely your guys!"

"Thanks for your help," Chief Vega said. "I'll be there first thing in the morning. We'll bring a couple of patrol cars. We'll drive them back over the border."

The next morning Chief Vega walked into the Toronto Police Department. Ken and Mark Cruise were waiting for him in a cell.

Chief Vega took the kidnappers and the rest of the ransom back to the Heights.

Joe Bush and the Cruise brothers were in jail. All three were charged with kidnapping. They were awaiting trial.

Chief Vega was very thankful to the Silvas. It was Lilia's tip that led them to the Cruise brothers.

Antonio was shocked that his shop teacher was involved. Ken

Cruise had been a good teacher. What went wrong? Antonio would have to wait for the trial like everyone else. Meanwhile, Coach Rome took over shop class. And Rafael got his father's present finished in time.